# The Misadventures of Millie

## Rodney & the Legendary Cricket Family

MilliE

# The Misadventures of Millie

## Rodney & the Legendary Cricket Family

Rebecca Heishman

TRINDIE
PUBLISHING
www.trindiepublishing.com

LCCN: 2014941751
ISBN:  978-0-9835204-7-4
Printed on acid-free paper in the United States of America

This book is dedicated to
all of the rescued dogs
who have flooded my heart with
the only unconditional love
I've ever known.
Though my life's goal has always been
to be as pure of heart as they are,
I continue to fall short in my efforts.

But that doesn't stop me from trying...

# Foreward

When Becky (Rebecca) asked me to write the foreward for her second book, I was honored. Through the power of the internet, Becky and I have become great friends—as much as two people who live nearly 1,500 miles apart can be. We are both dedicated dog-lovers and avid writers.

By virtue of the fact that you are holding this book in your hands, I'm guessing you already have a fairly strong interest in dogs and their well-being.

Dog lovers are a breed apart (no pun intended) from others. Most of us prefer the company of our canine companions to that of the human variety, paws down. We talk to our dogs as though they are capable of engaging in conversation; we share our food with them; we give them their own place on the furniture and in our hearts. These things are normal to *dog people*.

We understand each other and Becky Heishman understands *us*.

This will become even clearer to you as you make your way through this book. You will learn what I have learned in the past year or so...that Becky Heishman *gets you*.

She's one of you.

Within *The Misadventures of Millie, Rodney & the Great Cricket Family Rescue*, Becky artfully translates the signals she feels from her own (real life) dog, Millie, into a wonderfully entertaining manuscript that will touch you. The lovable character, Rodney the bachelor mouse, will make you question yourself the next time you discover a mouse in your home.

*The Misty Neighborhood* is an awesome place to hang out and you'll want to come back—again and again. You might even feel as though she wrote the book just for you. You will definitely look forward to her next book. It's been said many times but bears repeating: Becky writes *children's books for adults*. Her imagination is wonderfully childlike and refreshingly positive.

*The Misty Neighborhood*...you'll not find it on a map...it exists in the hearts of dog lovers everywhere.

Thanks, Becky, for showing us how to open our hearts enough to pass through the gates of *The Misty Neighborhood*.

**Tim Baker – Author, Flagler Beach FL**
**www.blindoggbooks.com**

# Praise for Rebecca Heishman

"Author Rebecca Heishman and I share many things. We are proud Hoosiers, we are writers and we share a love for nature. But one of the most important things we share is the love we feel for our companion animals. Rebecca's writing reflects the passion she feels for animals in need. If you love animals, humor and dog wisdom, this book will fulfill your needs."

**MARY CUNNINGHAM**
*Author of WOOF: Women Only Over Fifty,*
*Cynthia's Attic Series (Young Readers),*
*The Adventures of Max and Maddie (Tweens)*
*and mom to a sweet rescued dog named Lucy*

"Rebecca Heishman's writings and imagination are precious! Rodney is so adorable that he makes you want to write politicians worldwide and ban the use of inhumane mouse traps (*we're working on puppy mills, Millie!*). Rebecca's ability to read a dog is so precise that every time I read one of her books, I want her to come over to my house and tell me what my dog is saying."

**LAUREN HOWARD**
*President, Piece of My Heart Rescue*

"I would love to share with you how amazing I think Becky is. She is a wonderful advocate for rescues. The writing of her books and donating the proceeds is making it possible to help the less fortunate animals. I have personally received books from Becky to donate to different rescue organizations here in San Francisco for use at auctions to raise funds."

**ROCHELLE (SHELLY) SMITH**
*Animal Rights Advocate*
*Owner, Pooch Park Wear - San Francisco, California*

"Rebecca Heishman's passion for animals is clear and the Floyd County Animal Rescue League is delighted to be one of the many organizations she has graciously supported through her writing. Mrs. Heishman reached out to our organization in order to be a part of our 8th Annual Pet Lovers' Gala. We were so excited to have her set up during the event and were absolutely wowed that all profits from the night were donated to us.

We are grateful for her and her giant heart and hope she inspires others to be as kind and giving with their talents."

**ANDIE KYLE**
*Service Rep, Floyd County Animal Rescue League*

"Rebecca Heishman writes with a heart that's as big as the world—because her topic is her passion. *The Misadventures of Millie: Rodney & the Legendary Cricket Family Rescue* is dedicated to '...*all of the rescued dogs who have flooded my heart with the only unconditional love I've ever known...*' and within those first few pages, we understand why Rebecca has become such an impassioned advocate. We *see* life through the eyes of Millie, the Heishmans' own rescue dog; we laugh at her escapades and cry right along with Millie's human parents whenever something goes wrong; we enjoy Millie's interactions with Rodney, the house-mouse and The Cricket Family that share her space. Most important of all is *we believe* a dog—this dog, Millie—can talk! By the end of the book, we've become every bit as impassioned about rescue dogs as Rebecca—even me, an old cat lady! So please step into *The Misty Neighborhood* and enjoy! This book will warm your heart, whether you are young or old, and I'm sure you will be reading *The Misadventures of Millie* over and over and over again."

**SUSAN M. TOY**
*Author of Island in the Clouds*

"Rebecca Heishman is an amazing writer! The stories about her rescue dog Misty (and now Millie) are truly unique. These books are such a benefit for so many people of all ages. There are no words that can explain the way we feel about our pets. These funny books explain how pets see their people. The love they feel for us, the hilarious situations we have with them and the confusing reactions or emotions they show—somehow Rebecca puts their emotions into prospective for us. The proceeds from the sale of her books are donated to animal rescues and shelters. I would like to personally thank her for everything she has done for the pets in our community. Thank you so much, Rebecca!"

**PATRICIA ARMSTRONG**
*Director of Animal Adoption Network, Inc.*

"It has been said that 'a person who has never had a relationship with an animal has part of their soul unawakened.' Rebecca Heishman has a beautiful way of sharing this special relationship. Her writing reflects her soul's awakening."

**CHARLYNN BRANDT, DVM**
*Hillside Animal Clinic – Floyds Knobs, Indiana*

"Rebecca Heishman, who is fondly known as Becky, is the author of *The Misadventures of Millie*. A few years ago our library held a health fair and Becky shared a table at this event with the Clark County Chapter of the American Red Cross' Pet Therapy Group. As anyone who has read *The Misadventures of Millie* knows, this story is one of pure love; that this little dog finally found her forever home with Becky and her husband, William. This pure love permeates every aspect of Becky's life, from the work she does with animal welfare & rescue to donating the proceeds from her book sales to various pet organizations—in particular the aforementioned Pet Therapy Group. Becky is a shining beacon in our midst and every person who meets her is warmed by her presence."

**HARRIET GOLDBERG**
*Public Services Librarian*
*Jeffersonville Township Public Library*

"Becky is an inspiration to animal advocates and writers everywhere. Her books are fun to read and hard to put down. When she isn't writing she works tirelessly with animals, animal charities and fundraising events. She has personally donated her time and books to two charity events I have personally been involved with this year. The animals couldn't have a louder more loving voice in their corner."

**JOHN A. PASCUCCI**
*Author of Jethro Guardian Angel*
*Director of Promotions @Kritters.org*
*An Animal Non-Profit Organization*

"What could be more comforting to a young child than sitting down to read about a special pet who provides humor and laughter and creates many memories for a family as well! My grandchildren, great nieces and nephews have thoroughly enjoyed Becky's writings of Millie's adventures."

**BECKY ECKART**
*Retired school counselor*

"Becky Heishman is one amazing person. Her concern and work and all-out effort in animal welfare/rescue organizations are legendary. She has turned a beautiful little dog book (*The Misadventures of Millie*) into a national phenomenon. Her popular book blossomed into a full-scale series—the second book now out and, we hope, is just one of dozens more to come. What a lot of people may not know about Becky Heishman is that she donates every dime of her royalties from books sales to those very organizations that help those little dogs and animals in need. Every time one of her books is sold, another little animal somewhere is helped. She's a dog whisperer, of course, but she's also an animal support angel to boot. *You go, girl!* Those little dogs need you, as do many other critters out there in distress."

**LEE PENNINGTON**
*Screenwriter, poet, teacher and author of numerous books, including "I Knew a Woman" and "Thigmotropism"—both of which were Pulitzer Prize nominees*

"Rebecca Heishman is an avid promoter for animal rescue and adoption. She provides regular updates on Facebook for animals who need our help. *The Misadventures of Millie* series reflects this as she tells stories of a lovely dog who found a home. During the previous year I worked on the Quillective Project supporting no-kill shelters and believe Rebecca captures the spirit of our work. Her public events raise funds for animal welfare and rescue groups. Truly an author to support and a cause to remember."

**BEN DITMARS**
*Author of Night Poems, Haiku in the Night and contributor to Four Paws (The Quillective Project)*

"If reincarnation is real, I hope I come back as a dog. Specifically, I hope I come back as Rebecca Heishman's dog. I (and every dog lover!) cannot help but feel warm from the joy that Rebecca's tales radiate. Rebecca is grateful for the 'lift' writing gives her. I am grateful Rebecca discovered her gift and shares it so delightfully."

**DALE MOSS**
*Retired Indiana columnist for The Courier-Journal in Louisville, Kentucky and now writes a weekly features column for The News and Tribune in Southern Indiana*

"Many authors talk the talk, but Rebecca Heishman also walks the walk! She tirelessly agrees to book signings in order to generate additional proceeds for various regional animal welfare/rescue organizations. Her Millie, a rescue dog, has inspired her to help the countless others like her who are in need of forever homes. It may seem like a small act, but her generosity makes a difference in the lives of canines and felines."

**JO ANN SPIETH-SAYLOR**
*Editor of The Corydon Democrat*

"A simple Facebook message brought me to Rebecca and her writings, while they are not the writings the public would expect an adrenaline-driven MMA fighter/vigilante dog-rescuer to read, they have opened my eyes to the parallel worlds for which Rebecca and I share. While Rebecca escapes the cruelties of the real world and her disease through her stories of The *Misty Neighborhood* and *Millie*, I myself escape the cruelties of what I see and my own diseases through the gym and my fights in the cage. No matter who you are, you deserve an escape—these pages offer that escape through *The Misadventures of Millie*. Thank you to Rebecca Heishman for sharing this escape with me and for being an angel and voice for the dogs."

**GORDON "SHOTGUN" SHELL**
*Mixed Martial Arts Fighter/Independent*
*Cruelty Investigator/Animal Rights Advocate*

"If you remember the cartoon Calvin & Hobbes, I swore the creator was a VERY PRECOCIOUS six-year-old kid because he (Bill Watterson) captured the little boy so well. I'm beginning to think you (Becky) were a Chihuahua/Doberman in a prior life! I so look forward to the Millie stories. Please keep them coming! We all tend to anthropomorphize our pets and Becky captures perfectly what a little dog who thinks she is a Doberman would say if she could talk. Millie is so cognizant of her onerous duties as guardian of the neighborhood, and particularly porch patrol, and outwitting her loving human parents, as well as learning to tolerate the "Fluffhead" Poodle who has taken up residence in her home. Every time Millie talks about the "Chunky Monkey Starvation Diet" the vet prescribed, I can't help but giggle. I would love to meet Millie in person!"

**STEPHANIE CHODERA**
*Villa Park, Illinois*

# Acknowledgments

The Misadventures of Millie evolved from a community Facebook Fan Page entitled *Misty-the-Dog and Friends* (www.facebook.com/MistyTheDogNeighborhood)

I launched the page in 2010 in order to escape the ugly realities of multiple sclerosis, a mysterious disease that turned my life upside down. It even cost me my livelihood as a hospital staff nurse. I was convinced that before it was over...it would cost me my sanity.

My Facebook community page became a bright spot in my day. I launched it when my sweet old Misty, an elderly beagle/corgi mix, was still living. She was funny, feisty, playful and my husband and I adored her. I began writing daily adventure stories, told from Misty's point of view. My followers on Facebook responded favorably to the stories. On days when I skipped posting a story, incredibly, I was met with postings from my readers wondering where 'their story' was!

I was delighted.

Writing my stories gave me purpose and a sense of community. I could still communicate with people, even if those people were on a Facebook page. I could focus on something besides my disease.

My Facebook family grew and grew.

Misty died from kidney failure at the age of sixteen.

My Facebook family grieved right along with my husband and me. These caring people from all over the world became a part of my daily life. I want to acknowledge their kindness and their unflinching devotion. I thank them every day for being the anchor that kept me grounded when the days were dark and I thought my life was essentially over.

Misty was a rescued pup from a nasty puppy mill in the hazy blue mountains of rural Kentucky. My husband and I were led to the puppy mill by an ad in our regional newspaper. The first time we saw Misty and her five-week-old litter-mates, they were wallowing in a soggy cardboard box on a leaky porch in the rain. Their bellies were engorged with parasites. They'd been weaned way too early and were being forced to subsist on soggy adult dog kibble. We hastily gave the man our thirty dollars and fled the stark reality of that terrible place.

As we were leaving, we saw the pups' beagle mother chained to a doghouse in the yard. She was standing in a mud hole with rain pelting her eyes. But as dogs are apt to do, even in such horrific situations, she wagged her tail at us when we looked her way. Like most abused dogs, she was still looking for the good in people. The only positive thing we can say about that place is that a few days later, due to complaints from witnesses like us, the puppy mill was shut down by authorities and the dogs were taken into rescue.

Misty was and always will be my heart dog—that once-in-a-lifetime beloved dog that captures your heart when they're living and takes a hefty chunk of your heart with them when they go.

Even though she's gone, Misty is still my muse. I write the Millie adventures with her memory still fresh in my mind.

Our little Millie is special in her own right. A seven-pound ball of little-dog frenzy, attitude and angst, she is a Chihuahua/miniature pinscher mix. She is also a rescued breeder dog. While still a pup herself, Millie had been forced to have puppies. After the first litter, her body reacted with a false pregnancy and the backyard breeder labeled her as no longer profitable.

He dumped Millie at an animal shelter.

Millie is scarred. She harbors a fear of men. She was wary of my husband for many months after we adopted her. Sadly, but thankfully, my husband is now her only male, human friend.

Millie is a survivor because a kindhearted animal rescuer saw her in the animal shelter and recognized the beauty of her spirit. Mille was sick with kennel cough, malnourished and markedly underdeveloped for her age. Her rescuers healed her, loved her, and we were in turn blessed to find her soulful black eyes peering at us from the pages of Petfinder.com. (www.petfinder.com). My husband swears she was calling for him to come and get her.

The most amazing thing about Millie, and all the dogs who come from backgrounds like hers, is their remarkable ability to forgive and the unexpected ability to live only in the moment. They are capable of wringing every shred of joy from every moment of every day. Their spirits are not broken by past heartache. And, for some unfathomable reason, they continue to see good in the human race. Dogs are filled with the dignity, grace and nobility that many of us flawed humans lack. It is my sincere belief that dogs have come to me as messengers throughout my life, though I did not always recognize that at the time. I have learned life lessons from every dog I've ever loved. I now truly believe these wonderful creatures came to me as angels in disguise.

So, I decided to adopt Millie's attitude toward life. *And guess what?*

It's working for me.

Millie never looks back at the bad times. She focuses only on the here-and-now. To her, it doesn't matter what happened during those miserable days-gone-by. What really matters to Millie are the adventures she has today.

*Shhhh*...in a quiet, reflective moment we become aware that animals speak a beautiful language which can strengthen us in our human lives, if only we are wise enough to listen...

# Allow Me to Introduce Myself

I am a 64-year-old woman.

Like most of my peers, I've experienced the many emotions and life experiences women my age have encountered. My life has been full. I've known great love, great sorrow, personal loss and heartbreak. I haven't missed much. I've lived and I've learned. Life has been delectably sweet and at times incredibly difficult. My soul has soared with overwhelming joy. I've known crushing heartache. My heart has been enveloped in grief I never dreamed possible. I'm proud of who I am and all I've been through. I wouldn't have changed a thing in my life. Like all of us people of a certain age, I am the result of my experiences, good and bad. I am a survivor. Everything I have experienced has made me the strong woman I am today.

I am also very much in tune with current events and I make a point of knowing what is going on in the daily news. I refuse to allow myself to be left behind. I stay informed. I demand that of myself. I refuse to hide from what is going on around me—be it good or horrific. I care about people and I care about our world.

But here's the thing: I'm fed up with the negativity that cloaks our world today, and the many people and events wrapped up in that negativity. So, I've decided to live the rest of my days here in *The Misty Neighborhood*—a magical place that only exists here in my heart, my mind and my home. I created this place a few years ago in order to escape the uglier parts of the world. I made *The Misty Neighborhood* my sanctuary—my peaceful retreat where no one can harm me. All the beautiful memories of the beloved people and pets I have loved and lost still live in *The Misty Neighborhood.* Nothing can take them from me. I step into *The Misty Neighborhood* on a regular basis to recharge my childlike imagination and allow my heart to heal in the perfect peace, solace and tranquility of this imaginary spirit-healing place.

In The *Misty Neighborhood*, there is no pain. No strife. No negative thoughts. There is harmony amongst the creatures living here. In *The Misty Neighborhood*, all humans are kind and the animals are loved.

Goodness prevails.
Apathy doesn't exist.
Every story has a happy ending.

The sanctity and beauty of Mother Nature is respected and revered. No animals ever suffer neglect or abuse. Pets never go hungry. There are no puppy mills. Every puppy and kitten has a future. No animal, wild or domestic, is unwanted or unloved or mistreated. There are no animal rescue groups, simply because none are needed. *The Misty Neighborhood* is where we would all want to live, if life was fair, hearts were pure and all of our childhood dreams became reality.

My idealistic childhood dreams of a perfect world never materialized. I'm sure this resonates with almost everyone. The fact remains that within the beautiful part of our world, filled with good works and humanity, there is also sadness and negativity all around us.

But let's not dwell on any of that.

Like me, you now have a place you can go to escape...*The Misty Neighborhood*, filled with wise, delightful and insightful characters.

I can't wait to share my imaginary world with all of you. Step through the gate into *The Misty Neighborhood*, get to know Millie and her friends, embrace them and allow them to embrace you. And by all means join in the fun!

There is never a bad day here.
Every creature is free to live and love.

Everyone is free to live the life they were destined to live—in a perfect world. Here in *The Misty Neighborhood* only one rule exists, so before you step through our lovely gate and into the beauty this happy world offers...

Leave your worries at the gate

You may pick them up when you leave, if you must. While you're here, you will have no time or need for worry.

You will laugh.
You will smile.
And I'll bet you will shed a few happy tears, too.
So, come on in.
Listen to the animals.
Smile for a while.

Welcome to the Misty Neighborhood
Love Lives Here

# Millie Meets Her Match

Millie is standing beside the clothes dryer, intently looking behind it. The tip of her shiny-wet, black nose is shoved into the crack between the back of the dryer and the wall of the laundry nook in the pantry. As usual, she's overwhelmingly frustrated. She is unable to do anything but stand there, stare at Rodney and sniff.

Rodney likes it this way—Millie hates it.

Rodney intentionally sets things up in his apartment in such a way that Millie is unable to touch him. She's actively sniffing the air all around him, obsessed with the different smells that surround an old bachelor mouse. Today, along with his natural woodsy mouse aroma, Rodney is exuding the delicate fragrance of a combination of spring rain and dirty-damp-sweat-sock, and Millie loves this. One of Dad's fluffy white socks is heaped into one corner, lost forever to that mysterious world of vanishing laundry items Mom talks so much about. Millie often reflects on how fortunate Rodney is that Mom is such a lousy housekeeper. She entertains visions of Mom someday dragging out the vacuum monster, shoving its long, vacuous snout behind the dryer and sucking up Rodney's perfect little world. Millie doesn't understand why she finds the vision of that destruction so satisfying. It could have something to do with the perpetually smug countenance on Rodney's uncompromising face.

Rodney is a control freak and Millie hates competition.

Dad's sock is surrounded by carefully placed dust bunnies and impressive chunks of dryer fluff of all sizes and hues, which Rodney uses as tables, couches, chairs and footstools. One of Mom's freshly laundered blue washcloths from the bathroom—the fancy ones with the sunflower-yellow stripes, long ago lost from human view, serves as a comfy support for Rodney. It exudes a relaxing fragrance of lilac and warm summer breezes. Without a doubt, Rodney is the luckiest mouse in the world.

He's got it made.

His apartment is a virtual palace of plush comfort and lazy-mouse decadence and style. Like a king on his throne, he's reclined in an upright position, arms crossed, with paws clasped human-style across his rotund belly. He relaxes on his thick pink mattress of dryer fluff that rests atop the washcloth. His head rests on a lavender-colored dust bunny.

Rodney looks at Millie with that familiar expression of imposed tolerance on his whiskered face. His whiskers are twitching. They do that when he's thinking. His beady little mouse eyes are sleepy.

Rodney is the epitome of old-mouse laziness and, frankly, Millie is jealous.

She doesn't understand why everything is so easy for Rodney when everything is so difficult for her. He has the run of the pantry. He can hop from shelf-to-shelf with little effort. He dances among boxes of Cheerios, bags of cookies and whole loaves of aromatic fresh bread. He flaunts his ability to shimmy up walls and around woodwork. He leans against bags of Fruit Loops and boxes of salty crackers, taunting Millie with his impressive physical abilities. He can even visit The Cricket Family in the basement whenever he wants. All he has to do is slither under the basement door and disappear. Millie hates it when he does that and Rodney is well aware of her frustration. Millie has never been one to doubt the wisdom of Mother Nature, but she'd give anything to be able to do the things Rodney does so easily. Most days it's good to be Millie, but not when she's watching Rodney flaunt the fluid motions of his lithe and nimble body—and an old body at that.

Those days are infuriating.

"Go away, Millie. Leave me alone. I don't have time to listen to you today. I need some sleep."

Rodney is exhausted.

He is so glad to be holed up here in his apartment—the only place he's safe from Millie's prying eyes, reaching paws, that ever-intrusive dripping nose and the incessant demands on his time and energy.

She stalks his every move.

She dominates his time.

She's needy and unsettled and bored.

Rodney's nights are filled with scrounging for food to keep himself alive, while Millie and her humans are sleeping. His days must be reserved for sleep. Nocturnal living is difficult. While the rest of the world sleeps, Rodney is out there working. Skimming walls in the dark of night drains an old mouse's energy. Days spent sleeping here behind the dryer allow him the only peace he can find in this huge, rambling, roofed human abode, with its many floors and levels, craggy nooks, dark hallways and creaky stairs.

And then there are those haunting, gigantic, wooden pieces of furniture with animal-like claw feet that menacingly loom over him in the nighttime shadows. Why would humans have furniture with claws? What would be the purpose of such an abomination? Monstrous claw-footed chairs with arms and backs, dressed with antique lace doilies, gray with age, sit before soaring windows draped in heavy velvet that makes him sneeze when he climbs to the curlicue curtain rods.

Here behind the dryer Rodney can escape into a world that no mouse on the outside could even imagine. In this comforting space, delightful fragrances envelop him like a hug from Mother Nature herself. He simply doesn't understand how objects behind this dryer could possibly smell like flowers and the warm sunshiny days of spring, filled with heady lavender and a strong odor of pine.

But they do.

Inappropriate fragrances linger around this massive human abode on all levels and in every room. Sometimes he closes his eyes and imagines himself transported back to his childhood days of sunshine, tall grasses and massive clumps of blooming roses and pungent gardenia. He sees his mother's beautiful face again, her whiskers twitching with concern for her little ones' welfare and safety. The treasure-trove of fragrance here in his oasis behind the dryer is his favorite thing about living here. Everything in a human abode smells like something other than what it is. Human clothes smell like morning dew and peony petals, candles smell like peaches and cherries, and gingerbread reminds him so much of his old counter-surfing days with his mouse family. Bed linens and towels smell like verbena and the apple blossoms from the spring seasons spent in the gardens of his youth. Rodney has vivid memories of the garden he grew up in. Everything back then was as it should be. He and his brothers and sisters scampered together in the beauty and joys and openness of the earth. His mother was still alive. He was a young mouse with hope for the future. He had yet to experience the miseries of survival or the ravages of old age. His legs didn't hurt then and his teeth were still sharp. And all was well in his world.

Then the killings started.

The massive poisonings those many seasons ago claimed the lives of his entire colony.

Humans are a vicious species.

For reasons known only to the humans themselves, the only good mouse is a dead one. Within the short period of a couple of sunrises, everyone Rodney had ever cared about had been killed. The only reason he was still living was because he had gone exploring while everyone else in

6

his family ate the poisoned food. Defying his mother's rules, he had left the confines of the garden. He and his siblings were supposed to stay close to their mother's side. Always the disobedient one, Rodney had slipped under the garden gate and ventured out to explore the forest beyond. While he was nibbling on delicious mushrooms and attempting to climb ridiculously high fern fronds, his family members were dying off one-by-one.

When Rodney returned to the garden, he was met by a sight that would be burned into his memory for all time.

A big-footed human unceremoniously swept his dead family into a dust pan. His mother was gasping her last breath as her searching eyes disappeared from his sight. He knew without ever having to be told that she had allowed his siblings to eat their fill before taking a morsel of the food for herself. Rodney also lived with the reality that his mother's searching eyes were probably searching for him—the son who never followed her rules and always caused her worry.

He now had to live with the thought that his mother's last moments were spent worrying about him. He had always caused his mother to worry. And, for that, he punished himself his entire life.

The bodies of his kin were dumped into a huge bin at the back of a garden shed. Rodney stood alone, watching, his heart filled with awe, despair and anger at the brutality of the human species. He had survived only because he had rebelled. Since that day, Rodney walked his own path.

He followed no rules.

He answered to no one.

He was his own mouse.

He traveled alone.

For Rodney, there was no other way.

He ventured out into the world on his own after the deaths, seeking some semblance of family. There was none. Only one other family member had survived the poisonings. Marvin, a cousin on his father's side, was said to be living at the river park, far away, competing with the river rats for refuse left by human picnickers.

Marvin was lost to the streets.

Asphalt and concrete were all he knew. Rodney had never lived on the streets. He had known only the sweet life afforded a mouse who was fortunate enough to have been born within the beauty and solace of nature. Rodney had spent his youthful days cavorting with his brothers and sisters in a vast and luxurious garden. Together, with their mother watching protectively in the dewy grass below, they had shimmied up and down the long, thin branches of the golden forsythia when it bloomed. They always had shelter from the rain. They knew protection from the sun. They lived in peace, family harmony and they had love in their hearts. Back then it was lovely to be a mouse.

Life certainly had changed.

The realities of the world had hit Rodney squarely in the whiskers. The garden was turned into an asphalt wasteland by the human who killed his family. Nature disappeared right before Rodney's eyes and from then on he spent season-after-season running from danger. The threat of death was always around him. The brutality of the streets, the bitterness of winter, the scorch of the heat from the greasy asphalt in summer and the never-ending threat of sure death from the monstrous, starving street cats who increased in number as the seasons wore on. He had no idea where all the cats came from, but they were everywhere in this brutal city full of humans with their giant, metal, rolling modes of movement.

Humans never walked, Rodney decided. They rolled from one place to another. The humans were constantly in motion, rolling from place-to-place in huge, roaring, steel cages. Many a mouse lost his life, his body flattened under the wheels of those massive rolling cages. Rodney himself had experienced a couple of near-misses. Humans were a lazy lot. They were even too lazy to walk on perfectly good legs.

Finally, Rodney found this house.

He was old and tired and the streets had taken their toll on his health. He didn't have much time left here on the earth, he was sure of that. Just as he knew he would see his beautiful mother's sweet face again one day.

Rodney was tired—tired of life.

He wanted to coast his way through the rest of it, and this big old human abode afforded him comfort from the storms of life, whatever they might be. He was ready to hunker down and enjoy what life he still had ahead of him. He wanted calm. He wanted quiet. He wanted peace before he died. He truly believed that he'd found all those things.

Then along came Millie...

Rodney never dreamed that the life of the modern-day house-mouse could possibly be this hard. Modern conveniences like Ziploc bags, twist ties and Tupperware containers left many a house-mouse yearning for the old days. There were nights when the only sustenance he could scrounge up was some flour dust that Millie's mom had spilled from a canister on the top shelf of the pantry.

Rodney hates canisters.

Canisters and aluminum foil were two of the worst things to have ever happened to the house-mouse of today. Rodney is old enough to remember glorious nights spent surfing rustic wooden countertops for scrumptious delicacies, lightly covered only by soft linen tea towels smelling of earthy lye soap and fragile rose sachet. He often reflects upon stories told to him and his brothers and sisters by their grandparents. Tales of great feasts. Nights and days of lavish banquets, the tables laden with sumptuous mountains of foods displayed on easily accessible plates and platters for entire mouse communities to enjoy. Warm, fruit-filled pies cooling on windowsills. Tall, coconut-covered cakes displayed grandly on crystal stands. Magnificent wedges of salty yellow cheeses spread, row-upon-row, alongside plump, roasted chickens, their platters swimming with grease. Bountiful, gravy-slathered roasting dishes piled high with rich, succulent meats, beckoning to any mouse brave enough to risk being seen by prying human eyes.

In those days of kitchens run by human women who actually cooked, the reward was worth the risk. There were tiered stacks of cookies on colorful plates, rich and aromatic with butter and vanilla. Cinnamon, clove and nutmeg permeated the air. Back in those days, life for an intelligent house-mouse, well-trained by his mother, was one long, decadent, ongoing feast.

But those days were nothing but memories for Rodney. He'd found disappointment in this place. The dream he had of peace in his old age had faded away.

Humans in the old days were not as devious as they are today. There were no impermeable food containers. Cracker boxes are impossible now, especially for an old mouse with bad teeth. And Rodney has aborted all hope of finding crumbs on the floors.

Millie gets to them first.

He tried gnawing his way into plastic cookie packages. It's impossible to do. He wonders how even a human, with his magic paws, can claw his way into these noisy, crinkly, plastic fortresses. So much has changed in the world of food storage. Life these days is difficult for an old bachelor mouse.

Rodney's hopes of remaining an independent, self-sufficient mouse, the same as he's always been, are dashed. He had anticipated a peaceful retirement, far removed from the asphalt and the incessant stalking of the cats. Human abodes are magic to mice, for the simple reason that they are impervious to temperature fluctuation. How the human species avoid the chill of winters and the scorching heat of summers is a true mystery to the rest of the species of the earth. Perfect air temperatures seem to follow the humans wherever they live. The human species knows nothing of what it means to be a victim to the extreme temperatures of the outdoors. That is why, whenever a street-mouse becomes a house-mouse, it's almost impossible for that mouse to leave. Even living with the reality that the mouse is under the same roof as their mortal enemy doesn't inspire it to depart—because physical comfort is addictive.

*Why be cold when you can be warm?*

*Why be hot when you can rest in the coolness of a human house—cool, fresh air wafting over you at every turn?*

Comfort like this is surely worth some risk.

But, for Rodney, things had hit rock-bottom (again). The food situation was bleak and he was considering returning to the yard to search for sustenance. He would of course have to weigh his chances of survival in a yard plagued with hungry, stalking street cats.

*Could he run fast enough on his arthritic legs to elude their stealthy muscles?*

He knew he couldn't. And, at his age, and in his failing state of health, he wouldn't last long in the brutality of the changing seasons. It was so hot outside. He had flashbacks of his burning hot paws, blistered from the smelly, greasy asphalt he was forced to run on. These days his thin skin was no match for that physical torment.

He had no idea what to do.

In the meantime, Rodney still had Millie to contend with...

Millie's glistening nose is still jammed into the crack behind Rodney's apartment wall, and she continues to sniff him like prey. That habit of hers is intolerable to him.

Millie is so annoying.

Everything in life is a trade-off. Rodney is well-aware of that. His trade-off for getting to live here in the physical comfort of this massive abode is dealing with Millie on a daily basis. When he discovered this place, the pantry was to be his haven. He wasn't seeking a relationship with any other animal. He'd had his fill of the insecurities of having to deal with complicated relationships. Rodney had always been a loner, more out of necessity than by choice.

He certainly hadn't wanted to personally know a dog. Dogs are a couple of steps above cats, but not as clever, cunning or intelligent. It isn't hard to outwit a dog. What you see with a dog is pretty much what you get. Being manipulated by this dog flies in the face of everything Rodney and his honorable ancestors had ever stood for. His blessed mother would be so ashamed of him right now. She didn't raise her boys to grow up to be bossed around by dogs.

"Millie! I told you to stop that sniffing and go away. I was up all night scrounging for food. I don't feel like entertaining you. I'm tired."

"But, Rodney—I got nuffin' to do. I was hopin' we could talk for a while. Mom and Dad are out to lunch. I'm bored."

"Go pull one of your mom's magazines out of the rack and rip it. That always makes you happy."

"I already did that. I chewed up a coaster, too. I don't know what else to do."

"Take a nap."

"I'm not sleepy."

"Well, I am. Have some respect for an exhausted, hungry old mouse. *Please*. I had a rough night. All the food in this house is locked up tight. All my searching was for naught."

"You were searching for what?"

"Oh, never mind. You wouldn't understand."

"Well, looks to me like you could gnaw your way into some of the stuff in this pantry instead of layin' 'round here on your back, Rodney. We could share. We could work out some kinda deal. That box of Ritz crackers has been calling to me ever since Mom put it up there on that top shelf. You have no idea how hard it is for me to look at that box every day, wif pictures of crackers all over it. That box is torturin' me. You could take them mouse teef of yours and bust into that box, and we could have a party. I'd cover for you while you was workin' on it. You can climb—I can't. I think we're wastin' our time around here. There's good stuff here for us to eat. We just gotta make a plan. Your teef, your legs, your talent for climbin' and my brain. A perfect setup! Whaddaya think?"

Rodney sat halfway up. He was mildly interested.

"Millie, you're rude and self-centered and spoiled. It is totally unnatural for a mouse to be fraternizing with a dog. The only reason I tolerate you and your invasion of my privacy is that you are being fed by the humans on a regular basis. You tell me you want to be my friend. If that were true, you would care that I'm practically starving here, and yet you continue to eat regularly and get fat. If you truly want to be my friend, leave me some kibble in your bowl every night. If you can do that, I will try to help you with projects in the pantry during the day.

I might be able to roll some of the smaller packages off the shelves. You could break into them and we could share the contents. A few pieces of kibble left in your bowl in the evenings would be a step in the right direction if you're serious about maintaining a relationship with me. If you give a little, I will reciprocate."

"You'll what?"

"Never mind. I keep forgetting your vocabulary is limited."

"Look, Rodney, I may not be sophisticated like you. And I don't know big words, but that don't mean I'm stupid. You don't need to talk down to me like that. I'm not a pedigreed dog. I grew up rough, wif nobody to teach me manners. You need to know my story, then you'll understand why I'm the way I am. I'm not stupid—I just never had chances to learn. I was used as a breeder dog by a human who didn't love me. I had puppies so he could sell them. Then he dumped me in one of them places where humans take dogs they don't want. A kind human saved me from that place. Then I came to live here wif Mom and Dad. I never knew love like this existed between a dog and her humans. Yeah, I guess I'm a little spoiled, but I do my part around here. I've made it my life's work to protect my two humans, this house and all the humans and animals here in The Misty Neighborhood. So, you don't need to get snotty wif me, Rodney. My life has worth now because somebody loves me."

"Misty what?" Rodney started, then thought better of his question.

Rodney peered out of his window-to-the-world. There was a large crack around the dryer vent directly to his right, leading to the outside. It gave him a panoramic view of the yard. He watched as two of the cats ambled through the grass in search of unsuspecting victims. He realized he had to make this thing work with this annoying dog if he expected to survive. He had spent his whole life evading the fangs of those huge, furry, feline monsters. In his youth, he'd had nightmares of glowing yellow eyes in the dead of the night, staring down at him as he slept. He simply couldn't go there again.

He knew if he returned to the outside world to hunt for food, he would end up being the hunted. He simply must swallow his mouse pride, deal with this canine simpleton and hope she would feel a twinge of compassion for him. He needed some of that dog kibble. Kibble wasn't a food he enjoyed eating, but in a situation such as this he could do worse. He preferred to go that route rather than return to the outside world and scavenge dumpsters and trash bins again.

"All right, Millie. I understand about your lack of sophistication. I get it that you had a rough life prior to coming here, but I want to know once and for all...are you willing to leave some of your food for me every day? If you don't, I'm moving to the basement with Calvin Cricket and his family."

"Aw, Rodney, you know how it is for me. Mom talked to Dr. Evans again and he told her I was still too fat. I'm on the Dr. Evans Chunky Monkey Starvation Diet again. Mom and Dr. Evans are tryin' to starve me. It's some form of animal cruelty brought on by Mom's blind admiration for Dr. Evans and that big toofy grin of his. Mom always giggles when she talks to him. It's embarrassin' the way she acts. I think he's got Mom under some sort of veterinary spell, and my health is bein' affected by it. I get very little food. I'm so hungry all the time. I don't know if I can sacrifice even one kibble nugget."

"Okay. That's your choice. I guess I'll spend my days in the basement. I've been eying that big couch down there. I could make a fine apartment behind it and the Crickets won't bother me. The Crickets are a fine species. They never ask me for favors. Unlike you, they simply allow me to live my life, free of aggravation."

"Rodney, pwease! Don't go down there. You're the only animal friend I got inside the house. I never thought I'd say it, but I'd miss you if you moved. The Crickets are no fun. All they do is chirp and hop around."

"Life is all about choices, Millie. You must decide what your priorities are—friendship or a few more nuggets of kibble. Unlike you, I don't have a bowl that magically fills with food whenever I need it. My species has never been fortunate like that. The very humans who keep you nourished every day of your life only want to see me dead. You know as well as I do that, should your humans see me here, I am nothing but another dead mouse. There will never be a human who will help me to survive. Mice have always been discriminated against—treated as a lesser species. The next time you're standing next to a bowl piled high with kibble, remember your starving friend behind the dryer. I'll become a skinny old mouse and you'll find me stone-cold dead from lack of nourishment. And you'll be the cause of it! You and your gluttony. I'll simply die here in this fuzz-filled, dust-ridden pantry. An old mouse like me deserves to come to a more dignified end. Don't you think?"

"That's not fair, Rodney. Food is everything to me. Once I get to eatin', I just can't stop."

"Done! I'll be packing. I can take my furniture with me. You've never done a thing for me, Millie. You're leaving me here to starve. Soon, you'll stick that big ugly nose of yours back here and find me dead in this bed. It's just a matter of time. I'm old, Millie. I have bad teeth and the misery in my legs. I can no longer run from the housewife's broom. If your humans ever found me here, they would kill me. My dead body would be swept out with the trash. My carcass would be lunch for those hateful, grinning cats."

Millie feels terrible.

She pictures Rodney's dead body stretched on that washcloth and it makes her feel bad in her tummy. That image is ugly to her. She resolves to be the kind of friend Rodney wants her to be. Rodney's the only animal of another species who has ever asked to be her friend. Even though she knows he has selfish reasons for wanting to do so, she still considers it an honor. And, maybe if she can do that, he'll help her raid the pantry. Millie resolves to leave kibble in her bowl for him.

She will.

She must.

She absolutely has to.

She can do this.

It will be very hard, but she has to be a dog about it. Big Brave Dobie would do this, so she must do it, too. Big Brave Dobie knows everything. If Millie did wrong by Rodney, Big Brave Dobie would know.

And she certainly must maintain a good reputation to please Big Brave Dobie, the greatest dog that ever lived and her hero and dearest friend. Mom tells everybody that Big Brave Dobie isn't real. Millie just lets it roll off her back because she knows the truth and that's all that matters.

"Stop! All right! I'll do it, Rodney. No normal dog would make a decision like this, but I've never been a normal dog. I'm different and I know it. I want you to live here in the house wif me. I'll leave you kibble. I will. It's gonna be the hardest thing I will ever have to do, but I'm Millie, I can do anything, so I'll do this for you. I've already had my supper, so I'll leave you some kibble in the morning when I get my breakfast. You can eat it while Mom takes her nap."

"All right. I'm going to hold you to this. If I don't get nourishment soon, I'm not going to make it. An old mouse like me can't live on flour dust and your dad's discarded peanut shells."

"Okay, Rodney. We'll put our plan into action tomorrow."

"All right. Now go away. Give me some peace. Conversations with you simply wear me out."

Rodney is so exhausted that he dozes off with Millie stretched out flat on the floor on her belly, paws crossed, still looking at him. As she watches Rodney drift off to sleep, she silently extends a paw into the crack behind the dryer. She wants to touch him while he's sleeping, but she can't. He has everything purposely placed just out of her reach.

Rodney can be so annoying.

Millie reflects on the damage she did to Mom's magazine and to that coaster she pulled off the coffee table. She feels ashamed. She doesn't know why she continues to do these things when she knows Mom doesn't like it. These relapses only happen when Mom and Dad go out. Why do humans eat at other places anyway when they can eat at home? If Mom and Dad never went out, Millie wouldn't get bored and misbehave.

An uninvited thought pops into Millie's head.

Mom is going to be upset when she gets home and sees the mess Millie made in the living room. And, of course, everyone knows who will get the blame. Millie isn't proud of what she's thinking. If she told Mom there was a mouse living in the pantry that comes out and chews stuff up when she's gone, maybe Mom would believe it.

Life is full of important decisions.

Millie closes her eyes. Soon she's dozing. The old mouse and the little black dog are sleeping, almost touching.

Dreams of the puppy mill days disturb Millie's slumber. These dreams come to her much too often. As always, she hears the sound of whining puppies...

*The air is frigid and damp and her belly is cold against the steel floor of the cage. She smells the mold on the concrete walls.*

*There is no color.*

*There is never any color.*

*Millie's whole world is gray.*

*The water bowl is empty, but that's nothing new. Her tummy hurts. Smells of rancid urine and soured, matted fur drift through the air. In the distance, dogs cry in the night. Their voices blend in a chorus of anxiety, loneliness and the restlessness that comes from being hungry. Throngs of voices are crying, whining, howling. As she listens with a shred of hope in her heart, she* trembles as one lovely voice rises above the rest, calling her name.

It's an angel.

Millie longs to answer that sweet, beautiful voice. Maybe she'll meet that angel one day, if she ever gets out of here. Maybe that angel is looking at her right now. Maybe the angel will come here to this cage and take her and the puppies away for good. Maybe Millie will somehow find her way out of this ugly gray world. There has to be more to life than the walls of cages...there simply has to be...somewhere...

...Millie longs to answer that sweet angel's voice, but words won't come. She can't find her voice to speak. She longs to tell the angel everything in her heart. If only she could get to that angel's soft fingers, Millie would kiss them. The angel would lace her fingers around the wire of this cage and maybe that would make all the difference. Millie's kisses are the only gift she has to give in exchange for a way out.

The angel's voice comes closer, becoming more insistent. It seems to be directed toward her, calling her name softly and lovingly.

Can it be?

Has the angel come for her?

Nobody calls her by her name—nobody. This must be an angel sent just for her. Nobody has ever cared enough about her to call her by a name—any name. The voice is

25

*like music to her soul...feeding it...and it's better than any sound she's ever heard...*

"*Millie!* Wake up, sweetie! We're home. Why are you sleeping there, with your nose behind the dryer?"

Millie raises her groggy head. She feels so tired.

"Mom!"

Millie jumps into Mom's arms. It occurs to Millie that she's looking into the eyes of the angel. This is heaven and Millie already lives here. She kisses Mom's nose then snuggles her head under Mom's armpit. It's the safest place in the world. She thinks she might just stay here forever, here in the shelter of these loving arms. Even in her dreams, Millie never imagined there would be days this good. Now she knows that angels are for real.

Miracles do happen.

She's living her miracle right now.

# Millie's Morning Prayer

The next morning, Mom's up early making coffee. All Millie has to look forward to is her breakfast of low-fat, low-calorie, low-flavor kibble. Standing here looking at this bowl full of tasteless chunks of nothingness, she decides that the next time Dr. Evans sits her up in his hand and grins in her face, she will pee in his hand. Right now, revenge sounds a lot more satisfying to her than this terrible, gray, odorless food. Some days it's easy being Millie...other days...not so much.

She prays to Big Brave Dobie that once she begins to eat he will give her the strength to leave some food for Rodney. She'd never left food in her bowl—ever—no matter how bad it tasted. She remembers how hunger felt in the breeder dog days. Even bad food is better than none. Leaving food in this bowl will be the ultimate sacrifice in her rescue-dog way of looking at life. Food is never to be taken for granted. Consume whatever you have available to you. There is no vision lovelier to a rescue dog than a bowl heaped with food. There is no sight more beautiful than that of kibble nuggets being poured. That clinking, jangling sound they make as they hit the bottom of the bowl is the music rescue dogs live for.

She prays fervently to the spirits of all the dogs who ever lost their fight for life—the ones who never knew rescue, the ones who never knew the love Millie feels now, and who never knew what it was like to have a friend living in the pantry who needed their help more than anything in the world. In memory of those lost souls, Millie will do this because, if you can't help a less fortunate friend, how can you possibly live with yourself?

With dignity and grace (and with the shadow of Big Brave Dobie looming proudly over her shoulder) Millie begins to eat.

# Don't Mess wif Millie

"William! Get the Buick out! Something's wrong with Millie!"

"What? What makes you think so? She looks fine to me."

"She didn't eat all her food. She left quite a bit of it in the bowl. Millie never leaves food in her bowl."

"That doesn't mean there's something wrong with her, does it, hon?"

"Oh, yes! This indicates some sort of health problem. This is the first time this has ever happened. Get the car. We're heading to the clinic. I want Dr. Evans to look her over. He'll get to the bottom of this."

"Mom! No! Not Dr. Evans! There's nuffin' wrong wif me—really. Nuffin' at all. I just wasn't hungry. That's all."

"That does it! She's sick, William. This dog is always hungry. She's a glutton. Nothing deters that gluttonous appetite of hers. It must be something serious for her to react in such a bizarre way. Go on, William, harness her up and get her to the car. We're wasting time."

"Okay, hon..."

"Wait a minute—let me look at you, Millie."

"Ouchie! Don't be so rough wif my ears. A pain in my ears is a real big pain. And stop pokin' me. I said I'm not sick."

"Her nose is warm, William. I think she might have fever. We'll have that checked when we get there."

"No! No! No! Not the stick up the butt! Pwease...I hate that, Mom. You don't understand...I...well...I decided to be a whole new Millie. I want to help you and Dr. Evans wif the diet. Yeah! That's it. I put myself on a diet. Doesn't that make you happy, Mom? I mean, isn't this what you wanted?"

"Did you hear that, William? She's talking crazy. This isn't Millie talking. The very fact that's she's trying to cooperate with me with the Dr. Evans Chunky Monkey Starvation Diet is a symptom. This is a total change in character. It's like a different dog talking. A change in behavior like this in a dog like Millie could be the harbinger of very bad news. This could be some sort of neurological issue. An emotional break like this could be the result of some type of systemic infection. Sepsis! I've seen this happen in people—changes in behavior came about as a result of a horrible infection. This concerns me greatly, William. Let's go. This could only get worse before it gets better."

Millie drops to the floor, flat on her belly with her hind legs kicked out in back. She then assumes the position that kept her sane when she lived in the hard steel cage...she covers her eyes with her paws. If she can't see what's going on, then maybe it's not really happening.

"I'll get the Buick out, hon."

"Okay, William. I'll have them do blood work while we're there—I'll insist on it."

"No, Mom! No! No needles!"

"Quiet, Millie. Don't exert yourself. I know what's best for you, sweetie. Stop being such a baby. We'll get to the bottom of this. Don't you worry. I think we might tweak your diet even more. Maybe this food isn't agreeing with you. The treatment could be something as simple as giving you more vegetables. Healthy vegetables like green beans, kale, broccoli. Nothing's too good for my little Millie."

"Vegetables? No! Rodney! Help!"

"Rodney? Who's Rodney, sweetie?"

"Never mind, Mom. You don't know him. You wouldn't understand."

"William, let's get rolling. We need to step it up. She's hallucinating now—yelping for someone I never heard of. She's delirious. Brain disease! That's a possibility. We'll need an MRI of her brain. She could be suffering from some sort of encephalopathy. Maybe an infestation of heart worms. That could prove fatal. We need to check for that. We must rule out everything. A dog that's not eating is a very sick dog. This is nothing to be taken lightly, especially in a case like Millie's. For a glutton like Millie to stop eating, there is trouble in the wind. Come on, William. Step it up."

"I'm driving as fast as the law allows, hon."

"I don't care. Speed. This is an emergency."

Millie is slumped in her carrier in the back seat of the big blue Buick, watching the trees zoom by in a blur. She knows what's coming. In no time at all, she will be sitting in Dr. Evans' big white hand, with his big toothy grin in her face. She will be forced to look up into his scraggly nose hairs again. Those long, twisted hairs always twitch when he talks. As usual, his breath will smell like grease, garlic and cheese. As much as she hates him, Dr. Evans is still the best-smelling human Millie has ever known. She'll have to get a few sniffs in, despite the anxiety of the situation. But the fact that Dr. Evans always smells so good won't make up for the assault on her body and loss of dignity that will come after his grinning and her breath-sniffing cease.

Millie has no use for Dr. Evans.

He ruined her life with the Chunky Monkey Starvation Diet. Her life has never been the same. No more biscuits and gravy. Or doughnut bites. Or scrambled eggs with cheese. No pizza crust. Pancakes are a thing of the past. Chunks of cheese are history. Dr. Evans has Mom in some kind of trance. Mom does his bidding, no matter what he tells her to do. As he requested, Mom is starving her. What's going on in Millie's house is abuse, pure and simple. Dr. Evans is a bad human—a very, very bad human.

This is the day she will pee in his hand.

And, sooner or later, he must be Millie-nipped. Her mighty fangs will nip him where it hurts. That long white nose of his will be a perfect target. Sitting in his hand will give her the leverage she needs to nip him, Millie-style. It will be a huge surprise for him. He always brags about how sweet and cute she is. When Millie gets done with Dr. Evans, he won't think she's so cute.

His nipping is coming and it's coming today.

# Millie Gets the Upper Hand

Millie is back home, lounging on the couch. Dad has retreated to the garage to escape the heavy mood in the house. Mom is quiet as she tries to get some supper together. Millie entertains no hope of getting even one little nibble.

Millie isn't proud of what she's done, but every dog has a breaking point. Somewhere between the CAT scan, the MRI, the blood-drawing, the belly-pokes and the anal probing, she snapped. That should put a permanent end to the ridiculous eye-to-eye hand-lift Dr. Evans is so fond of. He will never again hoist her up into a sitting position in the palm of his big white hand. Her mighty fangs will never again be that close to his delicate flesh. Sadly, she will no longer be able to sniff his breath to enjoy the remnants of what he ate for lunch. She never intended to draw blood, but she was overwrought and it just happened. She hadn't intended to break skin. She only wanted to nip him to prove a point. To make up for what she had done to the tip of his nose, she had tried to lick the blood off as it trickled down onto his snowy white smock, but he batted her away before she could help. Mom's face was ashen and her mouth was wide open. The look in Mom's eyes had made Millie feel bad about the whole situation.

But this had been coming for some time.

The well of frustration from the prolonged examination, on top of the built-up anger from her daily starvation, led to that moment. When Millie made her decision, and the nipping started, there was no turning back.

It was done.

Dr. Evans had been Millie-nipped.

It was over and she could not undo it.

She was grateful that she had not inflicted a full-force Millie-assault. That would have been deadly, and she had no intentions of killing Dr. Evans. All she wanted to do was instill a sense of respect for her in his psyche, and she accomplished that.

Sometimes a human needs to be taught a lesson.

Dr. Evans had to be taught that you can't keep messing with Millie and get by with it indefinitely. Dr. Evans has always disrespected her as a watchdog. Millie is not a toy to be played with. Simply because she is small, Dr. Evans does not take her seriously. Big Brave Dobie would never tolerate any of what Dr. Evans put her through today. She'd like to see Dr. Evans try to hoist Big Brave Dobie up in his hand like that. Now that would be something to see.

When they arrived home, Mom and Dad were quite confused to see that there was no kibble in Millie's bowl. It had been there before they left for the clinic. Rodney had obviously found it and filled himself up. Sometimes it's good for a dog to live with old humans. Old humans doubt themselves and their failing memories. Mom and Dad quietly whispered about it between themselves, looking bewildered. Mom went to the medicine cabinet to take an extra dose of the herb she takes to try to salvage her faltering memory.

Millie kept quiet.

Let them be confused and perplexed. Nobody must know about Rodney—nobody, ever. Millie is the only living being to know where Rodney calls home and she loves keeping secrets. Secrets are very powerful things. She is proud to have a mouse as her friend. She hopes someday she can tell Rodney about all the sacrifices she's made for him. He needs to know that she was being tortured at the clinic while he was at home eating her food. And then, maybe, Rodney will be proud to have her as a friend as well.

Anyway—she has plans for Rodney.

A whole pantry full of deliciousness is calling to her and Rodney is the tool she needs to delve into all the awesomeness in those bright-colored boxes and plastic bags full of munching adventure. With Rodney helping, there is no end to what dining adventures are in store.

# Not Eggs-actly the Plan

"Shove harder, Rodney! Hurry up! Mom and Dad'll be home any minute."

"I'm shoving as hard as I can, Millie. These eggs just won't budge. They're heavy."

The humans are out to lunch.

Rodney ventures out to explore the kitchen. He plans to do some counter-surfing while the humans are gone. He knows Millie will be napping on the couch.

Much to his chagrin, Millie wakes up and somehow senses that Rodney is out-and-about. How she always knows what he was doing was one of life's greatest mysteries.

Spotting Rodney inspecting an empty snack bowl Dad had left on the countertop, Millie calls to Rodney to roll a hardboiled egg out of the bowl full of eggs. Mom had left them there to cool. These strange-looking eggs were all brightly colored. Rodney has never seen anything like them. They are all the colors nature has to offer. Some even have stripes and flowers all around them. But, strangely, they still smell very good. He tries to break into the shell of one with his ragged teeth, but it's no use. There was a time when he could have broken that shell with his teeth, but like everything else in his youth that skill drifted away with the time.

"Rodney! I want one of them eggs. Hurry up!"

Using his arthritic shoulder as leverage, Rodney shoves against a purple egg with all his might. He feels a twinge of burning pain shoot through his neck. The bowl is deep and the egg is heavy.

The egg simply won't budge.

"Come on, Rodney. Mom and Dad will be home soon. Shove harder!"

Rodney has had enough.

"Millie, you simply expect too much! I'm small. I'm no longer strong. I'm only one. I hurt all over and you don't care. I have limitations that you have no respect for. The basement looks so good to me right now. I could still do my kitchen raids at night and rest in the basement during the day. And the best part of it is...I wouldn't have to put up with you! You'll be snoozing away with your belly full of lazy-dog kibble!"

With an added dramatic flair, Rodney shimmies down the cabinet, zips along the baseboard behind the stove and slips under the basement door. Millie is left standing in the middle of the kitchen—alone, confused, eggless and forlorn.

Rodney streaks down the basement steps. He's heading for the sanctity of the only place in this massive abode where pesky dogs and snooping humans seldom go. A lengthy vacation from the stresses of the top floors of this house will be a welcome change. He needs respite from Millie's whiny voice.

Above all else, Rodney needs peace.

That's something in short supply in this world full of Millie-drama. If Rodney ever had sympathy for any human (though he knows he never would), he'd feel sorry for these two old humans who are run ragged by Millie and her many demands. The old woman is in a constant state of frenzy trying to keep Millie satisfied. What that woman has yet to understand is that satisfying Millie is an impossible task. No one of any species could do it. But, the poor woman keeps on trying.

Rodney is taking his only way out.

He'll live in the basement and spend his last days with Calvin Cricket and his lovely family. Calvin's species is well above canines when it comes to integrity. The Crickets mind their own business. That's a concept Millie will never ever understand.

Millie is still standing in the kitchen.

She is uncharacteristically quiet. She's mulling over Rodney's parting words and she feels hurt and confused. One of the only things she knows for sure is that animals of all species are forced to live in a world of human domination. If animals are to survive, they must do it with their innate intelligence. Life seems to go smoother if all species get along.

Millie knows she needs Rodney.

And, whether he realizes it or not, Rodney needs her. Millie has lived in the human world all of her life and she knows that *humans are in charge of everything*. You live by human rules, or you live without all the things you need in order to survive.

# Millie Makes Thing Right

Mom's having her nap on the couch before starting dinner. Nothing much changes around here. Millie can come and go as she pleases when Mom is out of the way.

While Mom snores, Millie transports kibble chunks, as many as she can carry in her mouth at one time,   to Rodney's apartment behind the dryer. She wants them out of her reach. With a flick of her paw, she bats each one as far away from herself as she possibly can. She doesn't want to be tempted to sneak back here later to eat them. Desperate measures are needed right now for her to set things right with Rodney. He's spending way too much time in the basement these days and Millie's worried. He's tired of the living arrangements upstairs, and he's clearly upset with her.

Yes, she's had weak moments with the kibble-sharing. Her appetite got the best of her a few times and she left the bowl pretty much empty.

Rodney is pouting.

He's hanging out with Calvin Cricket and his hopping, chirping clan and Millie misses him more than she ever thought she would. She believes that one of the reasons Rodney enjoys being with the Crickets so much is that the Crickets are small enough to make him feel big. Looking down on crickets is probably a confidence-booster for someone as small as Rodney. Millie certainly knows that feeling. Everyone has looked down on her for as long as she can remember—everybody except Rodney, of course. All the humans she has ever known have rudely picked her up like a loaf of bread and carried her wherever they wanted her to go.

Such a humiliating feeling.

Tiny dogs with hearts as big as Big Brave Dobie should never be carried around. It's disrespectful to watchdogs everywhere.

Everyone living this difficult life needs someone to look down on—someone who makes them feel big and strong and powerful. Being with Rodney makes Millie feel strong and protective—and important in a way. The only other time she has ever felt like this was when she was taking care of her puppies. When her puppies were taken away from her, she had no one left to protect. Looking after Rodney kindled some of those old feelings from all those sleeps ago.

She has to dig deep and try to win Rodney back. The house is not the same without him in it.

Millie is confident.

She knows she can do it.

She's Millie.

And Millie can do anything.

Rodney's got no business down there with those crickets. He's supposed to be up here with her.

# Giant Concrete Wasteland

Rodney is relaxing on the big gray couch that takes up a large portion of one of the basement walls. He enjoys its musty smell. There is a whole big world down here for an old mouse to explore. The basement is so huge that he can rest here, elevated on his pillow, look straight ahead and not even see the end of this place. It will take time for him to take it all in. One day when he's feeling rested he'll skim along the walls and familiarize himself with its cracks, ruts and secret places.

He's settling in nicely.

This space is starkly-plain and ugly and unadorned and that's what he loves about it. There are none of the fussy decorations the humans upstairs are so fond of. Humans put their stamp on everything. Their lives are filled with too many things—things that are not important in life.

*Things!*

Many, many things.

Humans all seem to love things.

Down here, there are very few things. There are boxes filled with dusty old books, some rusty grease-stained skillets, stacks of cracked china, a lamp with no shade, a few broken toys and an old beach ball, half-deflated with faded stripes. Rodney doesn't miss the decorations from upstairs. If he were to be perfectly honest with himself, he doesn't miss Millie either. Not at all.

No sound down here, except for the occasional thump of footsteps on the floor above his head. Once in a while he hears Millie yipping. She yips for no reason at all, just to hear herself yip. Down here her yipping is muted, so it doesn't bother him so much.

Rodney is also growing quite fond of Calvin Cricket and his family. There is no angst amongst this species. The Crickets live their simple, peaceful lives amidst the stark plainness of this concrete expanse of gray. Many might dislike the quiet coolness down here. Some would even call this place gloomy.

Rodney loves it.

It's a far cry from the turmoil and chaos constantly going on in the rooms above his head. This dark, dank place, draped in cobwebs and blanketed in dust, affords him the tranquility he needs during the day.

Calvin and his family had come here unwillingly by way of a cardboard box. Prior to their unfortunate arrival here, the family of four lived in the grassy shadows of the big garage that looms over the asphalt driveway adjacent to this human abode. Grass was their carpet and the sky was their ceiling, as it should be for crickets living in the freedom of nature. Outside, they had enjoyed the beauty of Mother Earth. Calvin and his mate Harmony had intended to raise their two little crickets amidst nature for all time. But one day, when the children were still little, a tragic turn of events landed them here in what Calvin refers to as "this giant concrete wasteland."

Calvin plunged into a state of despair at the realization that his two children would never experience fresh air again. As far as he could tell, the children remembered nothing of life before they were brought here.

Heliotrope and Heath believe the whole world is made up of gray concrete. They know nothing of fresh rainwater or morning dew. They subsist on the meager condensation of dirty water droplets that ooze and drip from the moldy concrete walls. Over time, Calvin tried and tried to find a way out of here, but he's since given up hope. Windows here are bolted shut and hidden with dark coverings. There are no doors, save for the one many, many human steps above them, barely visible in the gloom. Crickets are not big enough to make their way to the tops of stairs built by humans. Everything built by humans is built for their convenience only. There is no consideration for other (smaller) species who might not wish to stay here until they die. So, Calvin and Harmony, Heliotrope and Heath, are lost for all time in this place, with no hope of escape. Calvin can only look up at the huge door above his head and dream of some way of being magically transported out of here, returning to the world of beauty he remembers so vividly and misses so much.

Calvin is sad for his children.

Sad for his wife.

Sad for himself.

His children will have no concept of true beauty. All they know is this. To Calvin, being here is not living, it is merely existing. He is tormented at being the patriarch in charge of protecting his family yet being devoid of any shred of hope of ever getting them out of this dismal place.

The only other living creature down here is an ever-menacing, long-legged spider named Seraphina. Her expansive showcase of webbing is a symbol of foreboding death to every cricket. A webbed masterpiece of doom dominates one whole corner of a deep and lengthy shelf filled with tall, smudged, empty canning jars and dusty old kettles. The web, delicate-looking, intricately-woven, and full and heavy with undulating curves, sways with Seraphina's impressive weight as she skims along, never so much as breaking a thread. She leers down upon Calvin and his family on the floor.

She makes sure she is visible to all.

The Crickets stay close to the bookcase. They've taken up residence under the bottom shelf. It's the only place Calvin and Harmony feel the children have a chance of surviving should Seraphina decide to come down to their level in search of a tasty snack. But, as children are apt to do, Heliotrope and Heath sneak out at times to explore.

Calvin and Harmony must be ever-vigilant at hustling them back to safety if they wander too far from their parents' protection. Like tragic trophies, Seraphina flaunts the decaying cricket carcasses from long ago, each enshrouded in a tight bundle of silvery thread. The bundles are displayed in a macabre border running all along the edges of the web.

Calvin's family is not the first family of crickets to come here. Sadly, they might be the last. Other cricket families had become trapped here and none of them made it out. In the deepest part of his heart, Calvin believes his family will eventually meet the same fate. He keeps this dread to himself.

To escape death, he knows it will take a miracle.

Here in this sad and cavernous world, there had been no miracles for them so far. Calvin and his family are continuously taunted by Seraphina as they look upon the drying remnants of the brittle, crumbling wings and broken legs of dead crickets she has entombed high above the bookcase for all the cricket world to see. These long-lost victims are a blatant reminder of Seraphina's power. Calvin now thinks of this place as his family's tomb. To him, Seraphina is not just a spider, she is the harbinger of death.

Calvin's greatest burden to bear is the blame he feels. He blames himself for everything. He blames himself for the fact that his family is here, and he believes that the trauma of how they arrived here has left its mark on Heath.

Heath is unable to chirp.

He is a perfectly healthy and robust young cricket who should have a bright future ahead of him. He is now old enough to be looking for a mate, but there are no other crickets here. Heath will have no opportunity to be his own cricket, with his own family. Even if there were prospects, a young male cricket will not find a mate if he is unable to chirp. That is simply one of the laws of Mother Nature.

Calvin blames himself for Heath's disability.

Calvin's lovely daughter Heliotrope is the light of his life. With her elegant long antennae, she is striking in appearance and sweet of nature like her mother. Harmony has never once blamed Calvin for the situation her children are in, but Calvin knows her heart is broken. Harmony's gentle, accepting spirit only makes him feel worse. There are days when he would welcome it if she yelled at him. But she never will. She plods through life the way he does...heartbroken and quietly accepting of the inevitable.

A reckless, adventurous decision on Calvin's part left his whole family without a future. On the day he'd decided to explore the garage, he had no idea he was leading his family to this fate. On a whim, he had encouraged them to hop into one of the many dusty cardboard boxes set there, unmoved, on the garage floor, for as long as Calvin could remember. That particular box had always looked somewhat interesting to him, so he led the family to the bottom of it for a family outing. Exploring was good for the development of little crickets. This would be a learning experience for everyone!

A learning experience indeed.

In that box, there were colorful cloths of all kinds, soft and warm and fluffy. It felt good to be crawling around amidst all that softness. Together they explored an old doll with part of her hair missing, potholders with grease stains, and all the way to the bottom of the box was a pair of human shoes with laces and scuffed heels. Shiny glass balls, with hooks and painted red and green, were intriguing to them as well. It was a veritable feast of human materialism and decay. Humans seemed to hang onto the strangest things, and they were certainly a mysterious species.

The Crickets were having great fun exploring, until their world literally shifted under their bodies. The box was moving and they were moving with it. Calvin chirped for everyone to lay low. The box was swaying. Their bodies shifted side-to-side as the box clunked along, the weight of the box's contents putting uncomfortable pressure on their small bodies. It was now totally dark inside the box and Calvin was terrified that he couldn't see his family. He was hiding in the toe of one of the shoes, hoping his family was unhurt. He was praying that the children were not afraid. He didn't speak, for fear of being detected.

Finally, there was a mighty thud, accompanied by a heavy impact to the bottom of the box.

Everything stopped.

There were human footsteps.

A slamming door.

Then nothing but stillness for a very long time. The Crickets ventured out into this stark, sunless underworld of silence. Heliotrope had a minor injury to one of her antennae. Harmony and Heath seemed unscathed, though they were all visibly shaken.

Thus began what Calvin considered to be the end of a healthy, satisfying life and the beginning of a father's worst nightmare.

# Mighty Mouse

Rodney has an idea.

His mind is made up.

He's going to help Calvin and his family escape. He knows he will have to make amends with Millie because it will take both of them to pull this off. He's going to have to suck it up. Hopefully, Millie can remain calm enough to help him put the plan into action. While he was lurking in the pantry one day, Rodney overheard the humans making plans for an annual summertime yard sale. Evidently, this is a huge event in The Misty Neighborhood that brings all the humans out in search of more things to store in their abodes. It's evident that the human race lives to touch and hold and covet more and more things. They simply can't get enough.

Millie's dad is now making trips to the basement after supper. Rodney and the Crickets hide under the bottom shelf of the bookcase, watching as Dad lifts and examines and sorts through the objects in all of the boxes which have rested there, unnoticed, for so long.

Now, in the wake of the almighty yard sale, there is great interest in these dusty items. Unlike species who crawl, fly, swim or walk on four legs, humans love to embrace, stroke, fondle, kiss, cherish, hoard, cling to and, yes, *love* objects that have no heart or soul—no blood or tissue—no fur or feathers—no scales or gills—no meaningful purpose. This shallow exercise causes other species to question the quality of the human race. If a human places such value on cold, inanimate, non-living objects, can the human species be trusted with the vast responsibilities they assume in the world? To the animal world, humans will forever be a species cloaked in mystery, and the validity of the power they hold over others in the world will always be brought into question.

# Millie and Rodney's Rescue Plan

Millie spends evenings in the basement with Dad while he animatedly sorts and labels and rearranges objects of all sizes, shapes and textures. Mountains of previously useless stuff suddenly becomes important again, receiving much attention. In fact, these objects seem to be more important right now than any other objects in the house. Millie manages to steal away from Dad and huddle in the corner beside the bookcase while Rodney and the Crickets hide under the bottom shelf. They have been holding impromptu meetings here, finalizing the rescue plans.

The big event is to take place in the morning.

Millie keeps her body flat and her chin to the floor in order to take part in the conversation. She stares under the bookcase with as much nonchalance as she can muster and listens to Rodney as he repeatedly goes over the plans with Calvin.

Millie doesn't want Dad to suspect anything.

The hard concrete is cold on her belly. She feels ridiculous and even a twinge of embarrassment. Millie is a reputable watchdog consorting with a mouse and a cricket. She's not sure how to feel about that. In her heart, she wonders what Big Brave Dobie would think if he knew what was going on down here. She isn't really comfortable being involved in such clandestine activity, especially when she does not stand to benefit in any way. She will go along with it to keep Rodney happy. She has absolutely nothing in common with crickets. She simply wants to get this job over with so she can get back to being a dog.

# The Misadventures of Millie

The space under the bookcase is very shallow. As small as he is, the tips of Calvin's antennae still brush the shelf above his head, though he has become accustomed to this kind of discomfort during his many efforts to keep his family out of Seraphina's line of vision. She is always on the lookout for prey. Spider food is at a premium down here and Calvin and his family do not wish to be temptation for her insatiable appetite.

Rodney is flattened on his belly under the shelf with the Crickets. He has avoided being seen by the humans in every part of this house for as long as he's lived here. He's accomplished this through sheer wit and determination. It hasn't always been easy and it certainly hasn't been comfortable. This situation is particularly unbearable. His ears are smashed down flat against his head and they're cramping. The concrete is cold and the pressure is great on his fat belly. His legs are bothering him and his neck is stiff. He is unable to turn his head.

Rodney is one miserable mouse.

Rodney knows that when humans see a mouse they will often scream out loud and take drastic, brutal measures.

Humans are crazy.

Rodney has never understood why giant human monsters who rule the earth feel terror at the sight of an animal the size of one of their toes. It simply doesn't make sense.

But tomorrow...at least his friends the Crickets will be free. That was something.

Calvin's grateful heart is full. He wants to hang his head in gratitude and humbleness for all the kindness shown his family by these two members of other species, but he can't even move to show his appreciation.

Nighttime is falling.

Dim and dusty light bulbs dangle bright and bare from the ceiling. Millie's human has completed his sorting. Evidently, he is satisfied with the contents of the boxes as they are at the moment. Hopefully, he and Millie will soon leave. Calvin and Rodney must tie up the remaining loose ends of the impending escape.

An escape box must be carefully chosen.

Tonight the Crickets must arrange themselves in the bottom of the box for transport in the morning. Safety must be the priority. Millie and her human would sleep through the night, as usual. Rodney and the Crickets would keep their regular nocturnal ways, nervously waiting.

After the humans and Millie go back upstairs, Rodney and Calvin must survey the contents of the boxes to select the one that will be safest for the family to hide in. If all goes as planned, Calvin, Harmony, Heliotrope and Heath will be going out of here the same way they came in. Once the plan is implemented, there will be no turning back. Calvin must explain the details to Harmony and the children. Each of them will have a role to play. Everything must be synchronized. There can be no mistakes. Timing is everything. Everyone must be on the same page for the escape to be successful.

This is going to be a very long night.

Calvin is fighting to remain calm.
The success of this mission rests heavily on his shoulders. He's never felt so much responsibility in his life.
He will stay strong.

He has to.

The welfare of his family depends on it.

His antennae are twitching with anxiety as he tries to keep the children calm. As always, Harmony assures him that everything will be just fine. He shakes his head in bewilderment, wondering what she ever saw in him, and he realizes that any strength he may be feeling right now comes from the faith she's always had in him.

For her, he will succeed.

Rodney and Millie and her human are gone. Rodney thinks it best that he spend the night upstairs in case he needs to discuss any further plans with Millie. The Crickets are alone here in the dark, except for the ever-present shadow of a very large spider, spinning, spinning, spinning.

The night has grown silent except for the reedy, raspy chirp of a very nervous old cricket. Soon a cricket family who has been gone too long will be returning home—God willing.

# Calvin's Choice

Morning has come.

Calvin is wide awake and giddy with emotion.

It's time to begin.

His stomach is churning and his antennae are twitching with excitement. In just a little while, his family would see the sun and be enveloped in fresh air.

Fear threatens to choke him.

He is honest with himself.

He would have been much braver in his youth.

He realizes that his courage is still back there with that brave young cricket that now exists only in his memory. As his life melted away with time, he had become accustomed to the mundane. It occurs to him that the monotony of his days had made him feel a little too safe. He had become oddly comfortable in the boredom— his lot in life—even though he knew it wasn't what he wanted, or needed, for his family or himself. Even the danger of Seraphina has become familiar. In a sick and distorted way, it had begun to feel safe.

At least within his life in the basement, albeit stifling and reclusive, Calvin knows exactly what he is up against every day of his life. There are no surprises. Even someone who lives in a prison eventually succumbs to the feeling of familiarity and acceptance. The wild abandon of youth has forsaken him.

Walking is safer than running.

If he runs, he risks falling.

If he falls, he might be hurt.

Dreams are now only something he looks back upon, with longing. His life is being lived in quiet reflection. Routine confused with peace.

*Has he tricked himself into believing that the safety of routine is all he needs to be happy?*

Now all of the talk of how much he wants to rescue his family smacks him squarely in the face when the dream looks as though it might actually become reality.

He is gripped with apprehension.

His youth is behind him.

The road ahead of him is short.

But the one thing Calvin knows for sure is that he still wants to live. He feels shame at feeling fear for his own life. He is fighting the urge to give in to his seeming fate and abort the rescue plans. He is an old cricket and not a brave one.

But he knows he has to risk it.

If it were for his welfare only, he would probably choose to continue to live in the bondage of this miserable place. He had settled into a mind-numbing boredom that he no longer had the inner strength to fight. If his life was the only factor, he would continue on the way things were. In a bizarre way, he had taken comfort in the fact that for as long as his family had been here—nothing ever changed.

But Calvin truly loves his family more than he loves his own life. There is only one decision to be made. He knows it is best that they all risk dying together rather than to settle for life in this dungeon of gloom. He and Harmony never wanted their children to settle for the mundane. They wanted them to experience all that life as a free cricket has to offer. Calvin will dig deep and he will find the strength to walk through that door of change. He must get his children back out into the world of earth and sky. They must learn to walk in sunshine and dance in the dew. They must stand under a rainbow and be astonished at its colors. They will play under falling leaves. They should know how it feels to stand amidst the beauty of rose petals, their antennae twitching with delight at the fragrances swirling around them. And perhaps his handicapped son Heath would finally learn to chirp. Perhaps the newly found, earthly beauty around Heath would stimulate him to become the healthy, virile cricket he was meant to be. If only Heath could learn to chirp, Calvin could die a happy cricket. A young male cricket unable to chirp is doomed to a life of loneliness. For a male cricket, chirping is everything. Heath's inability to chirp is a silent source of sorrow for Calvin. Like every father within the universe, the only thing Calvin wants out of life is for his children to be happy.

Calvin makes peace with his fear.

He has no choice but to make this work.

Calvin is ready.

Ready as he ever will be...

# The Box Transport Mission

The stars have aligned.

Millie and Rodney's plan is falling together in such a remarkably perfect way that all parties involved are of the mindset that the Great Loving Spirit must have had a paw in orchestrating the whole thing. Everyone has a role to play and they are up to the task. There seems to be perfect symmetry in the way all parties are reaching out in harmony to make it all work. The result is an exercise in pure genius—a choreographed display of organized magnificence.

The annual summertime yard sale in The Misty Neighborhood is underway, and without a hitch. This is a huge event that is peculiarly important to humans. They ritualistically pile gobs of their stuff in their yards to rid themselves of it, after bonding with those same items for a very, very long time. This odd custom is common to the human species only. Unlike species who fly, crawl, swim or walk upon four legs, humans are as enamored with getting rid of stuff as they are of hoarding those very same things. Yet another unsolvable mystery of the workings of the human mind.

Box transporting to the front yard begins just before daybreak. Dad's plan is to take all the boxes to the front yard then head on out with Millie to the McDonald's drive-through for their usual Saturday breakfast of sausage-and-egg sandwiches and fried apple pies. As Mom always says, "If the world was coming to an end on Sunday, William would go to McDonald's on Saturday with the dog instead of staying here with me." Mom was always right. Some things never ever change.

Millie and Rodney are quite confident in their plan. They expect things to go well because of the predictability of the two old humans involved. Calvin is not so confident. Millie and Rodney have nothing at risk. Their lives are not on the line.

As usual, Millie's dad plans to take the food to the river park to eat with his friends, a group of old humans who solve the problems of the world over hot cups of coffee and delicious breakfast goodies. At the river park, Dad's friends will open their colorful sacks filled with slabs of bacon on toast, dig into their boxes filled with stacks of pancakes smelling delightfully of butter and maple syrup, and unveil muffin-wrapped fluffy yellow eggs and melted cheese accompanied by sausage links dripping with grease. Millie loves these mornings more than anything in the world because Dad's friends are always so generous. Not one of them has ever been able to resist Millie-charm and Millie knows how to lay it on thick. She always eats well when she's hanging with Dad and his buddies.

Dad's really smart.

He never tells Mom our secret.

As Dad always says, "What Mom doesn't know won't hurt her."


Since Rodney can discretely have the run of the whole house, he serves as the morning's courier of messages between Millie and the Crickets in case something goes wrong and plans need to be altered, or possibly even canceled.  No assumptions will be made. Humans are notorious for changing their minds and the team must be ready to change plans on a dime.

Calvin and the family huddled throughout the night at the bottom of a box full of old table linens. Calvin hunkered down under the pile of damask napkins. Harmony and the children rested comfortably amidst the stack of white linen tablecloths and the red table runner with the Christmas trees on it. Upon inspection of all boxes, this one was the only logical choice. In any one of the others, the family would risk being crushed by a rolling barbell or a heavy glass vase. Even a sliding book could kill a cricket.

Calvin must protect his family at all costs.

# Heath's Hidden Power

At dawn everything in the house, top-to-bottom, shifts into high gear. Dad is in a rush to get the boxes out to the yard so he can be on his way to meet his friends. Millie knows that nothing will deter him from this. Dad keeps a very tight schedule. Millie is salivating just thinking about the McDonald's extravaganza.

Dad makes several trips up and down the basement steps, boxes in tow, the heaviest ones first. Millie dances excitedly near his feet every time he surfaces from the basement with another load. Anticipation is getting the best of her.

"All right, all right, Millie," he says. "One more box and we'll hit the road."

Dad rushes up the steps with the box of linens, hurries out the front door to the yard and flings the lightweight box under the oak tree, striking the bottom of the box on a large, distorted tree root that bulges out of the ground near the trunk.

The box hits that tree root with a mighty thud.

Millie winces as she remembers what's in that box.

The shock of the impact sends a strange sensation, like a lightning bolt, coursing through Heath's body. His antennae shoot straight up, shivering with an electrifying, newly found strength so powerful that his antennae lift the mound of raggedy old dishcloths right up off his head. He doesn't understand what's happening to him and he wishes he could talk to his dad.

But he can't.

The number one rule during this mission is that the Crickets are not to speak during transport. The safety of the family depends on their ability to remain silent.

Deep within Heath's chest, a newly discovered strength is building. He is overwhelmed by the power of what he is feeling. He vows to himself to remain silent, but the power building in his chest overwhelms him. It seems to be taking control of his body. Against his will, and from somewhere deep within him, a great sound erupts. A loud, robust, perfectly normal cricket sound! It reverberates all across the yard in the still of the early morning.

"CHIRP!"

A perfectly fine cricket chirp—its tones slightly muffled by the weight of a cavernous mound of fabric, fills the air.

"CHIRP!"

It happens again!

And again!

And again!

Heath simply can't stop it. Both fear and gratitude grip his heart. Some wonderful seed, dormant for much too long, has burst open with life, by virtue of the impact of the falling box. A young male cricket who'd lost hope of ever being normal emerges as a perfect specimen of cricket virility.

Heath can only pray that the humans can't hear his joyous, unrelenting chirping. As hard as he tries to squelch it, this spontaneous need to chirp simply won't be denied. From his spot deep under the stack of dinner napkins, Calvin is filled with emotion—a mixture of joy and dread. He can't believe what he is hearing. He wants to hop to Heath and tell him how proud he is at this exciting break-through, but he still can't take their safety for granted.

Millie had been right, of course. Dad is already backing out of the driveway with Millie riding shotgun in the passenger's seat. She's making nose art on the window, looking pleased to see the silhouettes of four very shaken crickets emerging from a box piled high with raggedy old linens. The sun is shining on their faces, and their antennae are quivering with delight from the breezes blowing through them. As Millie rolls by, Calvin flicks one antennae in her direction in a gesture of triumph and gratitude.

Millie's behavior through the car window is spastic.

Rodney, totally exhausted from the hubbub, retreats to his former apartment behind the dryer, where he knows he will remain for the rest of his life. He is an old mouse who savors his sleep and he's missed this place. It suits him. Millie is leaving with her human and for Rodney that is always an invitation for him to run and grab a nap.

He promptly stretches out upon his bed of dryer fluff and is soon dreaming of running on healthy young legs, nibbling sweet apple pie, rich with cinnamon and sugar, and looking into his mother's eyes. With the crickets now free, the basement no longer holds the appeal for him that it once did. He reluctantly, but resolutely, decides to settle into a routine of dealing with Millie on a day-by-day basis. After all, they are friends now, as inexplicable as this might seem. How could they not be friends after being embroiled in an act of espionage this intricate? He hadn't even felt the need to be there when the escape was going down. Millie was in charge now, and he knows she can handle it.

An old bachelor mouse needs his rest.

# A World of Hope

Millie is sitting on her official look-out bench on the screened-in porch out front. It's nighttime. Dad has gone to bed and Mom's in the back watching TV. The mighty oak tree looms over Millie and her porch, its shadowy branches reaching over her like protective human arms. The sky is blue-black with wisps of clouds scuttling across the moon. The air through the screens is cool and comforting as it kisses her ears and dances across her nose.

Rodney joins her, silently slithering along the baseboards of all the rooms, undetected by the humans. He slips under the foot of Mom's chaise just inches from Millie.

Millie and Rodney are both very happy.

It feels good to do good things. Their hearts are full and their minds are at peace. Just outside, crickets are chirping in the evening twilight. Two cricket voices rise above the rest. Those two distinctive voices soar into the sky from behind the tall bushes that border the foundation of the porch just below Millie's bench. The two voices, one raspy and reedy, the other strong and virile, chirp a father/son duet of celebration. Heath hasn't ceased chirping since his arrival to the world of earth and sky. From all over The Misty Neighborhood, crickets are chirping their songs of exultation.  Heath is on his way to becoming a leader amongst crickets and lovely female crickets gather 'round to hear him sing.

Calvin need worry no longer.

Heath has come into his own.

The Crickets are free of restraint, as they were meant to be. They are hopeful and astounded by the array of startling colors. Their starved eyes are overwhelmed by the beauty. The world is right again.

# Let There Be Light

The basement is now devoid of life.

One momentous morning, Dad again went to the basement, cleared out the junk, swept the dust away and opened all the windows to let the sunshine flood the basement.

Seraphina saw the light and followed it and no one has seen her since. Rumor has it that under a lush honeysuckle vine that takes up one whole corner of the backyard fence there appeared the most magnificently intricate spider web the world has ever seen. Witnesses spied a few spider babies scurrying along fences, teetering atop chrysanthemum blossoms and dancing in the dewy morning grass.

Nothing remains of the former inhabitants of the basement except for one neglected old spider web gathering dust. A portion the web dangles with a dry and aging cricket leg suspended from the edge. It is a sober reminder of what life was like before Millie and Rodney took matters into their own paws.

The Legend of the Great Cricket Rescue will live on for years to come.

# When Dog, Mouse, Crickets & Humans Align...

The Great Cricket Rescue required strategic planning, dedication, teamwork and the united paws of friends reaching out to help one another.

This story quickly became legend within The Misty Neighborhood. It will forever resonate through future generations of species living here. It is a tale of courage unlike any other. It highlights the fortitude of one old bachelor mouse, the keen intelligence of a mischievous dog named Millie and the devotion of a patriarchal cricket who risked everything for the well being of his family. When a legend like this is given wings, it is passed to future generations of walking, crawling, flying, swimming creatures—all of God's creatures. The heart of the legend holds a lesson in the survival of all. Even though we are all different, we can work together to create a peaceful world for everyone and celebrate our differences. We may look different from one another, we may not agree on all subjects, but a thread of love lives in all of us. Threads, when bound together, can create a beautiful, stronger fabric. From that fabric, we can weave a comforting cloak filled with love that falls upon the earth, dispelling fear and enveloping us all in peace. Amazing things happen when everyone works together.

# Love Truly Does Conquer All

And that, my friends, *(may I call you my friends now?)* is the tale of **Rodney & the Great Cricket Family Rescue** in The Misty Neighborhood. Rest assured that all species will be talking about it for many seasons to come. We hope you've enjoyed this tale of amazing courage and heartwarming community cooperation. We also hope you'll open your hearts and take a lesson from the wisdom of the animals. Take their teachings and use them to benefit your own life. Animals are teachers. They come into our lives for a reason. They don't stay long, but they stay long enough to capture our hearts and teach us many things.

If you want to hear their voices, you will.

They have much to tell us and much to teach us, but we must be still and listen in order to truly understand their message.

Goodbye for now from all of us here in
The Misty Neighborhood
Stop by often and always remember...
**Love Lives Here**

# The Misadventures of Millie Collection

*Rebecca Heishman's next book is a delightful collection of stories about some of her most beloved characters. Following is a sneak peek just for you!*

## Rodney's Journey

Rodney-the-Bachelor Mouse is restless. The walls of his apartment behind the clothes dryer are closing in and he needs to feel like a mouse again. Living the good life as a house mouse, with a nosy and irritating dog as his only friend, is taxing his nerves and giving him an itch to head out into the dangers of the city in search of Marvin, his only living relative. Marvin is said to be living at the river park many city blocks away. Rodney will set out on a quest with Twitch, his emotionally-damaged friend. Twitch's life changed forever when he witnessed the gruesome and bloody reality of his family's death. They perished in their nest under the grinding blades of a roaring lawnmower being pushed by an uncaring human.

Along his journey, Rodney meets a magical creature who has become a legend in the Misty Neighborhood—Big Brave Dobie—a regal and majestic Doberman who lives in Millie's imagination as her alter-ego. Or is Big Brave Dobie more than a fabrication in Millie's mind? The truth comes out. Rodney will learn that 'home' isn't always that distant place in your memories; that friends don't always look like you and family doesn't have to share your blood. Rodney will learn that home is where his mind is at ease and his soul is at peace.

Home is the place where love lives.

# Baxter's Last Dig

Baxter Beagle is a sweet, gentle and docile old dog who lives with his widowed human mom right in the heart of The Misty Neighborhood. He loves little human children more than anything, and all the delicious smells that linger on their hands. Human children smell like peanut butter and jelly, Pop-Tarts and gummy pink erasers.

Baxter's eyes are cloudy with cataracts. His muzzle is gray from age. Arthritis in his hips makes him waddle. He looks innocent enough. In fact, Baxter is downright lovable and he never meets a stranger.

But, Baxter has a notoriously criminal past.

Baxter is a digger.

He simply can't help himself.

He is a beagle who was born to dig and no fence can contain him. Baxter has created more havoc in The Misty Neighborhood than any other animal in neighborhood history—wild or domestic.

But things change for the better after Baxter's last dig. Even today, the humans continue to whisper amongst themselves about a mysterious occurrence that set loose a chain of events which would change the soul of The Misty Neighborhood forever. An incredibly beautiful story would be revealed, long buried and lost to time, that would touch the hearts of humans everywhere.

Friends come together to do good things.

Baxter finds his rightful place amongst the good dogs of the world and all will be forgiven when the citizens of The Misty Neighborhood finally learn the story of a magnificent dog named Baron.

# Animal Advocate Organizations

## Kentucky Humane Society

kyhumane.org.
241 Steedly Drive
Louisville, KY 40214
Beth Hobson, Director of Development
Email: bhobson@kyhumane.org.

## Piece Of My Heart Rescue

pieceofmyheartrescue.org.
PO Box 44
Floyds Knobs, IN 47119
Lauren Howard, President

## Animal Adoption Network, Inc.

aanok.com
Patricia J. Armstrong, Director
Laconia, IN 47135
Ph: 812-267-9608
Email: pjarmstrong70@aol.com

## Floyd County Animal Rescue League

floydcountyanimals.org.
Brad Bane, President
Dana Fisher, Vice President
PO Box 285
New Albany, IN 47151-0285

# Alley Cat Advocates

http://www.alleycatadvocates.org
Karen Little, President
3044 Bardstown Rd., #204
Louisville, KY 40205
Ph: 502-634-8777

# About the Author

A fierce animal advocate, author Rebecca Heishman descended from two of Indiana's earliest pioneer families where she grew up on an historic pioneer farm in Corydon, Indiana. The family home was built of logs harvested from the land and hewn by her father's family; the deed to the farm written on sheepskin parchment and hand-signed by John Quincy Adams. She still lives with a sense of that history and honors the work ethic which was the hallmark of her family.

*"I was a quiet, introspective little girl with a great love for nature and the outdoors. My years as a teenager were spent studying hard. My card from the local library in town was well-worn and much-loved. My father signed up for every book club and record club in existence, and my book choices were never censored. Our home was filled with music and I was allowed to appreciate art and free expression. My parents allowed my imagination to soar and my mind to be open to the world. My first dog as a young child was a beagle-mix named Rusty who bonded with me immediately. He had the huge brown eyes of the beagle breed and his ears were long, soft and floppy. He was gentle and sweet and he loved me unconditionally. Rusty was one of the many stray dogs my parents rescued from the country roads of southern Indiana. Rusty and*

*I were never apart and it was a great love affair. Not only did his life teach me the beauty of unconditional love, his brutal death taught me that all people were not kind. There was a farmer in our neighborhood who had a mean streak and Rusty had a habit of chasing tractors when farmers rumbled by our house hauling hay or pulling plows or combines. One afternoon my mother, brother and I were standing on our front porch when the mean farmer came speeding down the hill on his huge red Farmall, pulling a plow. When the noisy farming equipment was right in front of us, Rusty took off on his fast little beagle legs. Mom was helpless to stop him. He ran into the road and got very close to the huge back wheel of the big red Farmall, chasing, barking and baying, beagle-style. We watched in horror as the farmer intentionally swerved that wheel in Rusty's direction, striking him. Rusty rolled and tumbled on the asphalt and his body spun under the blades of the plow. The farmer drove on with a parting, menacing look in our direction. Rusty was able to stumble to the side of the road, where he died, cut and bloodied in the grass. My mother took my brother's Western Flyer red wagon, pulled it to Rusty's body with her two weeping children walking along beside her, gently lifted Rusty's body into the wagon and pulled it home. She never told Dad the details of Rusty's death. She was afraid Dad would kill the farmer. That was my earliest memory of animal cruelty. It was one of the many life lessons I have learned from my many years of loving animals."*

Rebecca, or "Becky" as friends and acquaintances know her, studied creative writing at Indiana University Southeast and at the University of Louisville. In 1986, she was one of three winners of the Kentuckiana Metroversity Creative Writing Competition in the Poetry Division—over 600 poems were submitted by creative writing students of all levels. In 2002, Becky was struck with multiple sclerosis and was faced with new challenges and an overwhelming feeling of depression that left her feeling hopeless. Life as she had known it was over. What she didn't expect, was to quite literally have her life saved by a dog...Rebecca now champions for abused animals and has made it her mission in life to rescue as many as possible. Her social media following grows daily (and sometimes by the hour!). It is her hope to extend her reach beyond her home state of Indiana (and nearby Kentucky).

Rebecca Heishman resides in the small town of New Albany, Indiana with her husband William and their two adorable pooches Millie and Luna. Married since 1975, Becky and William used to enjoy traveling the United States and Canada in search of scenic train rides, particularly the old steam engines, and even had the opportunity to ride some of them. They also have a great love of National Parks and have traveled to many of them over the years. The Heishmans are diehard fans of all divisions of motorsports. William is a 70-year-old athlete who bikes and walks every day and his adoring wife Becky says, *"If you ever pass through New Albany, Indiana, you might see a tall, silver-haired fellow on either a fancy-looking multi-speed bicycle or a cool red 50cc scooter. That would be my William. He is a big fan of professional cycling and follows the Tour de France. William and I are young at heart. After 38 years of marriage, we are still in love. People sometimes ask us how we've made it work all these years. We can only speak for ourselves, but when we look at one another today, we still see the young couple from 1975—as though we are frozen in time in each other's eyes. When I look at William, I see a handsome young county sheriff filled with devotion to duty and love for life. When he looks at me, he sees a pretty blonde girl with big blue eyes in hip-hugger bellbottoms and a halter top. We hold on to each other for dear life and we don't let go. Mature love is a soft and warm glowing ember that never grows cold. We love our home. We love our life. We love one another. We are not special. We are simple people living a simple life by choice. And we wouldn't have it any other way."*

# About the Illustrator

The talented illustrator, Daniel Mendoza, resides with his family in Henderson, Colorado. As many animal advocates tend to do, Daniel graciously agreed to donate a portion of his time to help get Millie's message out to the world—the result of which is a beautifully illustrated book that we know will captivate the hearts of many, many species. We are eternally grateful for kind souls like Daniel.

## Thank you, Daniel!

# Special Thanks

I want to thank Dana Grizzél of TrIndie Publishing for taking a chance on an eccentric lady with a penchant for telling stories about talking animals and insects. She saw my vision and made my dream come true. Her patience, caring and perfectionism with the project touched my heart and resulted in the exceptional quality of the book you are holding in your hand.

*Rebecca Hirshnier*

MilliE

www.ingramcontent.com/pod-product-compliance
Lightning Source LLC
Chambersburg PA
CBHW071326130626

46556CB00004B/1760